Amy Neally

To Nuremberg and Back

A Girl's Holiday

Amy Neally

To Nuremberg and Back
A Girl's Holiday

ISBN/EAN: 9783337292577

Printed in Europe, USA, Canada, Australia, Japan

Cover: Foto ©Andreas Hilbeck / pixelio.de

More available books at **www.hansebooks.com**

TO

NUREMBERG AND BACK

A Girl's Holiday

BY

AMY NEALLY

ILLUSTRATED

NEW YORK
E. P. DUTTON & COMPANY
31 WEST TWENTY-THIRD STREET
1892

CONTENTS.

LIST OF ILLUSTRATIONS.

TO NUREMBERG AND BACK.

A GIRL'S HOLIDAY.

— ◆ —

CHAPTER I.

AN UNEXPECTED PLEASURE.

ONE day in the early spring. Alice Winter came home from school, and, after the usual question at the door, "Is mamma at home?" rushed upstairs, and found to her great surprise that her papa was at home, talking very earnestly to Mrs. Winter.

When Alice came into the room. Mr. Winter stopped talking, and she wondered very much what they could have been talking about so earnestly, as all she heard was her papa asking, "Do you think we had better take her with us?"

"Why, papa! What is the matter? Are you going away? Are you sick? What made you come home so early?" were the questions which Alice gave rapidly, without waiting for an answer.

Mr. Winter said. "Yes. dear. I am obliged to go to Nuremberg. Germany. on business immediately; and mamma is trying to make up her mind whether it is best for her to go with me. She does not like to leave you for so long a time. and we do not think it wise to take you with us, when you are getting on at school so nicely."

"O papa. please take me with you. I shall learn just as much on such a lovely trip as at school. and you know I can take care of mamma, and keep her from being lonely when you are busy. O papa. please ask mamma to let me go. I should be so unhappy to stay without you, even with dear Aunt Edith. and I know there is where you would send me."

"Alice. dear. go to your room and get ready for dinner. and leave us to talk it over," said Mr. Winter. "My dear little daughter knows that no matter which way we decide, it will be as we think is best for all of us. You know it is as hard for us to leave you as it will be for you to let us go."

Alice left the room without another word, with her heart beating very fast from the excitement of it all.

The thought of going to Europe across the great ocean was a very happy one to a bright girl of fifteen who was studying all the time about the places she would visit and the objects of interest she would see, if her papa would only decide to take her.

Alice sat down by the window of her pretty room, and looked out on the village street, far away in the northern part of the State of New York. She wondered how the ocean looked, as she had never seen any larger body of water than that of Lake Erie, when she went with her mother to make a visit in Cleveland.

She also wondered if her state-room on the steamer would be as large as the room she was in; also, would she be sick, and how would all those

wonderful cities look; if they could be as beautiful
as the pictures she had seen of them.

Then she remembered that only last week she had
been studying about the quaint old city of Nuremberg. and wishing she could go there and see all
its curiosities.

Alice was startled by the dinner-bell. and could
not even wait to brush her hair, she was so anxious
to know what her papa had decided.

As Alice went into the dining-room with a very
wistful look in her deep-brown eyes. Mr. Winter
said, "Well, dear, we have decided to take you
with us. and as it is now Wednesday. and we sail
Saturday from New York on the 'Etruria.' you
will be very busy getting ready. and you must help
your mamma all you can."

Alice threw her arms around Mr. Winter's neck,
crying with joy, saying at the same time, "Oh, you
dear. darling papa. how kind and good you are. and
how I do love you!"

After kissing him again and again, she went to
her mamma and nearly smothered her with kisses.

Mr. Winter had never been abroad, though he had large business interests there, which had been attended to by a clerk in whom he had the utmost confidence. This clerk had been taken very suddenly and dangerously ill. Mr. Winter had no one else he could send, and found he must go himself and at once.

He telegraphed to the Cunard office for staterooms, and went home to tell his wife, hardly thinking she would go with him at such short notice, or leave Alice.

Mrs. Winter was not willing he should go without her, and soon decided not only to go, but to take Alice with them.

Alice could hardly eat any dinner, she was so happy and full of excitement.

The next morning Alice went to school to get her books and tell the wonderful news to her teacher and school-mates.

They were nearly as interested as she, for it was quite an event for any one to go to Europe from that quiet village.

It was decided then and there that all would be at the station to see her off on Friday.

When Alice went to her room she found there a new steamer-trunk marked "A. W." in large letters, and then she was busy indeed getting it packed and deciding what to take with her.

Mrs. Winter came in while Alice was almost in despair and said, "This is to be such a hurried trip you will need only a couple of dresses, but you must take all your warm wraps."

Alice laughed and said, "I do not think I shall need them in the spring;" but mamma said, "It is always cold at sea, and you will need your winter clothes."

Friday afternoon our little party started for New York, with the best wishes of their friends, who came to the station for the very last "good-byes." Alice even shed a few tears, but they were soon wiped away, and a happy face looked from the car window, which fortunately was on the side overlooking the Hudson River.

Alice had never seen that lovely river before, and naturally was delighted.

When they passed the Catskill Mountains it was
so clear she could see the famous old Mountain
House, and, beyond, the immense Kanterskill Hotel,
which seemed almost in the clouds, it looked so
high.

West Point was the next object of interest, and
Alice did hope she could go there sometime and
see the cadets do some of their drills.

When they were opposite the Palisades, which
stood up in their grandeur, with the softened
tints of the setting sun settling upon them, Alice
said, "I know I shall see nothing in Europe any
finer than that."

Very soon the tall spires and smoke in the distance showed that they were drawing near New
York, and after leaving the Hudson they followed
the pretty Harlem River, which makes an island of
New York City.

Alice was much interested in the bridges, there
seemed to be so many of them, and papa told her
that the one then in sight was the new Washing-
ton bridge, just completed. The next was High

bridge, which carries the water over the river into the city. When it was finished it was said to be the finest engineering in the country.

The next bridge was the continuation of the elevated railroad, and then came Macomb's Dam bridge, the oldest of them all, and used simply for driving and walking across, and looked, Alice thought, quite unsafe.

The pretty Madison Avenue bridge was the last they saw as they crossed their own bridge, and were soon in a tunnel which Alice thought would never end.

When they came out of the tunnel the train was nearly at the station, where the noise and bustle were very confusing, and they were glad to get into a carriage to be driven to the Fifth Avenue Hotel.

As it was quite dark, Alice thought it was like a glimpse of fairy-land when they reached Madison Square, with its electric lights shining on the trees, and all the bright lights around the hotel.

CHAPTER II.

NEW YORK FOR THE FIRST TIME.

MR. WINTER having telegraphed for rooms, found them ready for him; and on going down to dinner they were delighted to see the corridors and dining-room crowded with people, many of them public characters whom he could point out to Alice, who was so excited she felt the entire evening as if she were in a dream.

Of all the prominent men there Alice was the most interested in General Sherman, with his kind, rugged face.

The "Etruria" sailed at noon on Saturday, and Mrs. Winter and Alice spent the morning buying a few last things, such as a hat and hood and comfortable steamer-chairs.

At eleven o'clock a Fifth Avenue Hotel stage was at the door, and several people beside themselves

went in it to the steamer. The ladies had flowers
and baskets of fruit. and seemed so bright and
happy that Alice for the first time felt a little lonely
and homesick.

On reaching the dock there were so many people
going on and coming off the steamer. and pushing
each other. it was almost impossible to cross the
gang-plank and reach their own state-rooms.

Finally they found them. and. instead of nice large
rooms. they were so very small that Alice felt she
never could live in them for a week or ten days.
and the berths were so narrow she said. " O papa.
you can never get into one of those in the world."

"Oh. yes. I can." said Mr. Winter. "and perhaps
before we reach Liverpool I shall wish they were
narrower yet."

Mrs. Winter and Alice had one room. and Mr.
Winter was across the passage with another gentleman.

After settling their valises and rugs they went
up on deck to see the people. and also the last of
the city itself. Large baskets of fruits and flowers

in every shape were constantly being brought on board. and much to Alice's delight there was a large bunch of violets from her school friends at home.

She had been looking at the other people a little enviously. especially at a girl of her own age who had many friends to see her. and her arms full of flowers.

Very soon the gong sounded, and Alice, who had never heard one. put her hands to her ears to shut out the noise. As soon as the man had passed by Alice said. —

"What is that?"

"That is a gong. dear." said her papa, "and is now being used to notify the people who are not sailing on the steamer that it is time to go ashore."

The people who left kissed their friends hurriedly. and went down the gang-plank as if afraid they might be carried away. after all.

After the people were on the dock and the mail-bags had been put on the steamer. very slowly but surely the great steamer backed out into the river.

THE GREAT STEAMER BACKED OUT INTO THE RIVER. — *Page 21*.

Tugs turned her around. and carefully she steamed
toward the ocean. trying to avoid the many boats
moving about the river in all directions.

Alice was rather frightened, and thought they certainly would run into some of them.

Many of the passengers were still waving to their
friends, who were also waving to them from the
dock as long as they could distinguish it at all.

Very soon they could see the famous statue of the Goddess of Liberty, that holds its light so high in the air; then lovely Staten Island, with its green hills and fine houses.

The two forts, Hamilton and Wordsworth, which guard the entrance to the harbor, were soon left behind, and on the left could be seen Coney Island, with its large hotels and elephant and high elevator.

Suddenly, as they were looking at the largest hotel of all, the one at Rockaway Beach, the steamer stopped. Alice, rather startled, said, —

"Oh, dear! what is the matter?"

"They are going to drop the pilot," said her papa.

"Where?" said Alice. "In the water?"

"Oh, no," said Mr. Winter: "do you see that small boat rowing towards us?"

"Yes, papa. Will he drop into that? He never can; he will surely fall into the water."

Mr. Winter smiled and told her to go and watch from the rail, which she did, and soon saw the pilot go down the side of the steamer by a rope and drop into the little row-boat. where two men were waiting to row him to the pretty pilot-boat No. 4. which was quite a distance away.

The steamer started immediately. and in five minutes the row-boat was only a speck on the water.

"There is another hotel. papa. What is it?" said Alice.

"That is the Long Beach Hotel, and you will not see another until you reach Liverpool," said her papa.

CHAPTER III.

LIFE ON A STEAMER.

"COME, Alice." said Mrs. Winter. " we will go down to our state-room and unpack our trunks while we are in smooth water, for to-morrow morning it may be so rough we cannot get out of our berths at all."

Alice went with her mamma and helped put everything in order, but there were so few hooks and no bureau she did not know at first where to put anything.

Mrs. Winter decided to sleep in the lower berth and have Alice on the sofa, which gave them the top berth for a bureau. and they found themselves very comfortable.

Alice wanted to put some little things around to look pretty, but her mamma said, " No. dear, for if the ship rolls they will be all over the floor."

Alice laughed and said. "I guess the 'Etruria' never rolls enough for that ; she is too big."

"Wait and see." quietly said her mamma.

Mrs. Winter said. "Now we will put on our warm wraps and go on deck."

Mr. Winter had found their chairs and put them in a nice place. Just as they were being settled in them, the gong was sounded again. "That is for lunch this time." said Mr. Winter. "and I for one am glad, for I am very hungry."

On going to the saloon they were delighted to find that their seats were at the captain's table, and any one who has crossed the ocean with Captain Hains knows what a treat they had before them, if it should be a nice passage and he could be in his seat at the head of the table.

In the afternoon the ship rolled, and when dinner was announced Mrs. Winter thought she would take hers on deck. She was not sick. but was afraid if she left the air she might be. Mr. Winter and Alice went to the table. and Alice was surprised to see the vacant seats around the room. The racks were on

the table, so the dishes were held in place, but Alice
found it rather uncomfortable keeping her chair.

In the morning Mrs. Winter was too ill to leave
her berth, but Alice never felt better in her life. The
captain was so pleased to have her at the table to
breakfast he put her in her mamma's seat next to
him, and when she told him it was her birthday he
said, " You shall have a nice cake for your dinner."

After breakfast Alice went up on deck with Mr.
Winter, who put her in a comfortable place and
covered her up nice and warm. He went down to
see his wife.

The sea was a deep, bright blue, with lovely white
caps, and when the sun shone on them Alice could
see a rainbow on every wave.

Alice became tired of sitting in her chair, and went
to the rail to look over the side and see how pretty
the water looked as the ship cut through it. Soon
the young girl whom she had seen the day before
came up to her and said, " Have you ever crossed
before?"

Alice said, " No, have you?"

"Oh, yes. several times; and I do enjoy every minute. for I am never sick."

Alice asked her name. and she answered. "Nellie Ford. What is yours and where are you going?"

Alice told her name and that she was going to Nuremberg.

Nellie said. "I have never been there. We are going to Brussels. and it is such a beautiful city."

They talked on until the gong sounded, and agreed to meet again after lunch.

At dinner that night Alice found the cake which the captain had promised her on the table. After thanking him, she asked if she might send a piece of it to her new friend.

"Of course. my dear." said the captain. "It is yours to do with just as you please."

The second day was very much like the first, only Mrs. Winter was able to be on deck, and Nellie Ford introduced her to Mr. and Mrs. Ford, and they soon settled to a little party of six. as passengers on a steamer are very apt to do.

The two girls were together all the time, and

HOUSES OF PARLIAMENT. — *Page 37.*

joined in a game of ring toss with some more of the young people.

The days passed away, one very much like another — some pleasant, some stormy and rough, some foggy, with the whistles being blown every two minutes. Alice felt that she should be glad when she saw land again.

One night they met a steamer, and it did look very pretty all lighted up. The "Etruria" set off Roman candles, which were answered by the steamer, and Alice thought that was the most interesting evening of all, even more so than the night of the concert.

The "Etruria" made a very quick trip, and reached Queenstown Friday afternoon. Alice was writing letters in the saloon to send home, when suddenly the steamer stopped.

"Oh, dear, what is the matter?" she cried, jumping to her feet. A gentleman sitting near her said, "It is a fog, and as we are very near Fastnet Rock they do not dare to go on."

Soon a gun was heard in answer to the steamer's

whistle, and the gentleman said, "We must be right there now."

Alice went up on deck rather frightened, but as suddenly as the fog had settled upon them it lifted, and directly ahead of them was the straight rock rising out of the water like a sentinel.

The "Etruria" ran up her signal flags and then started on, and in three hours was off Queenstown Harbor, where the tug was waiting for their mails and the few passengers who wished to be landed.

CHAPTER IV.

A FIRST GLIMPSE OF ENGLAND.

QUEENSTOWN was soon a thing of the past, and when they went to their rooms the packing was finished, so that the next morning all the time could be spent upon the deck until they landed.

It was a clear, bright morning, but very cold and windy, when the steamer was left to take the tug. On leaving the tug, Alice and Nellie were very careful to each put her left foot first on the dock, as they had been told it would bring them good luck.

There was not much to interest our party in Liverpool except the docks, which of course Alice had been told were the finest in the world. After leaving the Custom House they were driven to the North Western Hotel, and the ladies and two girls waited in the parlor in front of an enormous soft-coal fire, while Mr. Ford and Mr. Winter went into the station, which joins the hotel, and engaged a compartment for London.

Opposite the hotel they could see St. George's Hall, with its two statues in front, one of Queen Victoria and the other of her husband, Prince Albert, when they were young.

Suddenly a noise of horses being rapidly driven was heard, and the girls ran to the window just in time to see the high sheriff's carriage of state being driven to the hotel to take him away to open court. It was very elegant, with its satin linings and the four beautiful horses.

The footmen stood up at the back of the carriage, holding themselves on by leather straps. Four men in uniform stood in the street and blew on trumpets until the sheriff was out of sight.

The girls thought it very interesting, but Mrs. Winter said, "A sheriff's position in England must be very different from that in America, where they usually go about in the quietest manner possible."

Mr. Winter and Mr. Ford came in and told them

it was time to get some lunch. A very nice one
they had, and Alice was particularly interested in the
table on wheels. with the joints of meat on it.
which was pushed about to each person to select the
cut of meat he liked.

Mr. Ford advised their going to the Hotel Victoria in London. as he had tried many others and
liked that one the best; so they had telegraphed for
rooms before starting on the two o'clock train.
All the party were in good spirits. and glad to be
on dry land.

Mrs. Winter and Alice did not like the carriage,
as it is called in England, as well as the drawing-
room car at home. but enjoyed every moment of
the journey.

England is like a large garden. every portion
being under cultivation; the fields are so green and
full of large, beautiful sheep grazing everywhere.

"O mamma. how much more lovely the hedges
are than our fences and walls at home!" said
Alice.

"Yes, indeed." said Mrs. Winter. "I have always

heard they were lovely, but I did not think they would add so much to the beauties of the landscape."

Harrow, with its school on the hill, was passed, and caused some interest to the girls. London was reached before they realized it, and they were driven to the Hotel Victoria in two four-wheeled cabs called "growlers"—why, they did not know, unless people "growl" at their lack of comfort in every way; no springs, narrow, high seats, generally dirty, and a worn-out old horse, whipped the most of the time by a very poor driver.

Their rooms were ready for them, and glad enough they were to get their dinner and go to bed to get rested for the following days, to which the Winters were looking forward with great interest.

NELSON COLUMN.

CHAPTER V.

A WEEK IN LONDON.

SUNDAY our party rested, but on Monday morning
they started for Westminster Abbey, hardly looking at anything on the way, though they went by
Trafalgar Square, with the high column erected to Nelson, which stands there so proudly, with its beautiful
lions made by Landseer lying so quietly at its base.

A pleasant morning was passed at the Abbey, and the Poets' Corner proved to be their greatest attraction, as it is with most Americans. The chair in which Queen Victoria sat when she was crowned was shown to them, but Alice said she thought it was a common-looking chair, and wondered why the Queen did not have one that was more imposing.

On leaving the Abbey they naturally turned towards the Houses of Parliament, and wishing to get even a better view, they walked part way over Westminster bridge, where they also saw St. Thomas's Hospital, situated on the Surrey side of the Thames.

The walk back to the hotel by way of the Embankment was very pleasant, with its large buildings one side, and the river with its boats moving up and down on the other, and the rumble of the underground railroad beneath their feet. On reaching home they were so tired it was decided to rest in the afternoon and visit Madame Tussaud's wax-works in the evening.

After dinner Mr. Ford said, "How would you like to go to the wax-works by the underground railway? It is not very far, if you think you won't mind the smoke and confined air. The station is very near, and we shall be left at the next building to the wax-works. I have been driven there and it only took about twenty minutes, so I think we can go by train in ten."

"All right," said Mr. Winter; "it will be a good opportunity to see how we shall like it."

Off they all started to the Charing Cross station. The girls did not like going down underground so far, but Alice said to Nellie, "I think I will not say much about it unless mamma does."

After passing three stations, Mr. Winter said, "This air is stifling, do you not think we are nearly there?"

"Oh, yes," said Mr. Ford. "I think it must be the next station."

When they reached it, it was not theirs, and Mr. Ford called out to the guard. "How many more stations before we reach Baker Street?"

The man looked at him rather queerly, and said. "Fourteen. Where did you get on the train?"

"At Charing Cross," said Mr. Ford.

"Oh," said the guard, "you have taken a train for the outer circle and come the longer way; some one should have told you."

The train moved on, and our party had nothing to do but sit patiently and try not to think how close and stifling the air was getting.

When they were once more in the fresh air Mr. Ford said. "Driving in cabs suits me pretty well, and that is the way I am going home, if I go alone."

There was not a dissenting voice, and after a very pleasant evening they had a lovely drive home in three hansom cabs, and it only took them sixteen minutes.

Tuesday morning was spent in visiting the Bank of England and St. Paul's Cathedral, where the young people and the gentlemen went upstairs to the Whispering Gallery.

They all went down to the Crypt, where are many tombs, among them those of Nelson and Wellington.

The great object of interest to them was the immense funeral car which was made to carry the body of the Duke of Wellington through the streets of London to his last resting-place.

The wheels were made from pieces of cannon picked from the field of Waterloo.

Mr. Ford took them to a quaint, old-fashioned place noted for its soups, for lunch.

In the afternoon the Tower of London was visited, and of course was of more interest to the Winters than to the Fords.

To Alice it was very realistic, it was so full of English history. She could tell her mamma much more than could the man, in his strange costume, who showed them around.

That night the ladies and the two girls were too tired to go out again, so Mr. Ford took Mr. Winter and they did a little sight-seeing on their own account.

Wednesday was given up to visiting the Buckingham Palace stables, where they saw the Queen's famous ponies that are only used on state occasions; and the South Kensington Museum, which they found very interesting.

TOWER OF LONDON. — *Page* 40.

HAMPTON COURT.

In the evening they went to the theatre, and Alice thought it very strange to go downstairs to their seats. The audience looked so much better than in America, as the ladies were in evening dress and the gentlemen in dress suits.

Thursday was a lovely day, and was spent at Hampton Court. They went on the outside of a coach, and what a lovely drive it was through Richmond and Bushy Park, with its wonderful horse-chestnut trees all in bloom!

The coach stopped at a little inn beside the river, where they lunched before visiting the famous court, once the home of Henry the Eighth, and presented to him by Cardinal Wolsey. It is now the home of certain ladies of small income who are alone in the world. They are selected by the Queen, and of course have only one portion of the palace.

The remainder is occupied as state apartments and a famous picture-gallery, beside a gun-room only second in interest to that of the Tower.

Friday was given to Windsor Castle and the Crystal Palace.

Saturday they shopped and visited the Royal Academy, where they saw a beautiful collection of paintings, and only wished there was more time to spend looking at them.

Mr. and Mrs. Ford decided to go with the Winters as far as Brussels, and as they were to start on Monday it was thought best to keep very quiet on Sunday.

Mrs. Winter said to her husband she wished they could stay longer in London, where every minute had been a delight; but he said it was impossible.

CHAPTER VI.

OFF FOR THE CONTINENT.

MONDAY morning was bright and clear, and Mr. Ford said. "This looks like a pleasant crossing of the Channel."

The ride in the cars to Dover was very interesting, and the view of Canterbury Cathedral was quite fine.

Quite a large boat was waiting for the train, and the water looked so smooth Alice said. —

"I guess the people who are sick crossing this Channel do not know much of ocean discomfort."

Like a good many travellers who see the Channel for the first time, she thought it must always be quiet.

It proved to be a very smooth trip, and only a little over an hour was spent in crossing.

The train left Calais fifteen minutes after the

arrival of the boat, and the gentlemen bought nice luncheons which were put up in baskets, — chicken, bread and butter, and a bottle of wine.

They found a good compartment, and away they went, eating their lunch and enjoying the views from the windows at the same time.

Belgium is called the garden of Europe, as vegetables are raised there for all the principal cities.

The country is flat and rather uninteresting to look at, but when one realizes that the willows which surround the farms are used by the women and children to make baskets which are sent all over the world it becomes very interesting.

The land is divided by water wide enough for flat-bottomed boats to be rowed about, that the farmers may till their land and bring home the products in them.

It seemed very strange to see women at work in the fields, but Mr. Ford said they would get used to that before they reached Nuremberg.

It was dark when the train drew in at the station at Brussels, and they took a stage marked

"Grand Hotel," and were driven through the principal street of the city. The shops were all lighted, and the streets and sidewalks full of people.

Outside the restaurants little tables were set on the sidewalks, and men and women were eating and drinking.

It was a sight the Winters had never seen, and it looked very strange to them.

"It is just like Paris on a small scale," said Mr. Ford.

Excellent rooms were ready for them at the hotel, as they had been telegraphed for by Mr. Ford, who was in the habit of going there every year.

They had a delicious supper, and Mr. Winter said. —

"That is the best meal I have seen since leaving America."

The ladies had found the cars very hard to travel in, and were glad to go to their rooms.

The next day Mrs. Winter was so thoroughly used up that Mr. Winter decided to stay in Brussels a few days for her to get rested.

The girls were delighted, as they had become very fond of each other and were dreading the separation.

BRUSSELS BOURSE

Mr. Ford had to go out on business, and Mrs. Ford said she would entertain Mrs. Winter if Mr. Winter would take the girls sight-seeing. They started on their walk in high spirits, and found such wide, clean streets, interesting shops, and large, handsome buildings.

The new Exchange just completed, and the Palace

of Justice, are two of the most magnificent civic buildings in Europe.

They were much interested in a lace manufactory. On the lower floor were women at work on the finest patterns. They were all ages, from twenty to seventy, and never looked up while their work was being examined.

When the girls were leaving the room, Alice laughed at some remark of Nellie's, and then every head was lifted and a sad smile came on each face for a second.

Mr. Winter bought two lace handkerchiefs for the girls to take as presents to their mothers.

Through the remainder of their stay in Brussels they had lovely drives in the beautiful park, visited the Palace of Justice, situated at the end of a long street, on a hill where there was a glorious view of the surrounding country for miles.

They also found that the picture gallery had a very fine collection —indeed, said to be the best in Belgium, and the pictures were beautifully arranged in schools and periods.

One day was given to the field of Waterloo, which they all enjoyed very much.

Alice felt so unhappy to be parted from Nellie that Mr. Winter finally persuaded Mr. and Mrs. Ford to let Nellie go with them to Nuremberg, as it would give her a delightful trip, and she was equally miserable to be left in Brussels without Alice.

It was decided to meet in Paris, have an enjoyable week together, and sail for home on the "Etruria" near the middle of July.

CHAPTER VII.

UP THE RHINE.

ON Monday, Mr. and Mrs. Winter and the girls said "good-bye" to Mr. and Mrs. Ford and started for Cologne in the gayest of spirits.

The trip was found very interesting, as they followed the Meuse River a great deal of the way. Between Liège and Verviers the country was wonderfully picturesque, with the pretty winding river, which they continually crossed, and little villages with the mountains in the distance.

The Meuse has been called the miniature Rhine.

Verviers is the last Belgian station, and Aix-la-Chapelle is the first town of much interest in Germany.

From the train there was an excellent view of the city, which has seen many changes since it was the favorite home of Charlemagne.

COLOGNE CATHEDRAL.

For more than three centuries the German emperors were crowned there.

It was growing dark as Cologne was reached. but the girls. knowing the cathedral was near the station. hurried outside to see it. and how wonderfully high and beautiful the noble great spires looked in the twilight no one can imagine who has never seen them.

Tuesday morning was spent in visiting the Church of St. Ursula (which is reputed to hold the bones

of eleven thousand virgins martyred by the Huns)
and the cathedral.

An excellent guide showed our party around, and
pointed out the beautiful windows which King Ludwig presented, costing eighteen thousand pounds.
English money.

The late King Frederick gave one elegant window,
at the end opposite the entrance.

On one side of the building were windows made
by Albert Dürer, considered Germany's greatest artist.

A large gold cross, presented by Marie de Medici,
and costing an enormous sum of money, Alice
thought was more beautiful than the windows.

On the way back to the hotel they met a company of soldiers who were singing as they marched
along. It seemed very inspiring.

Wednesday morning this happy party took the
train for Mayence up the Rhine, as the boats, they
found, were not yet running.

Alice and Nellie had been reading up the legends
of the Rhine, and could hardly wait to see its
beauties and wonders.

The Rhine was not reached until after leaving Bonn. The scenery was so pretty they did not miss the river views.

In full view of the train was the famous avenue of horse-chestnuts, three-quarters of a mile in length. There is a large university at Bonn, and many other schools. As many of the students in their different costumes came to the station and walked up and down the platform to show themselves, the girls were very much amused.

The city is also noted as being the birthplace of Beethoven.

As soon as Bonn was out of sight, the river was beside them. At first the entire party were disappointed, the river seemed so quiet, narrow, and sluggish, compared to the rivers at home.

However, that was soon forgotten as its beauties grew upon them.

They soon saw the Seven Mountains coming into view, and wished they could stay over one night to see the sun rise from the top.

Mr. Winter felt he must hurry on, as they had

spent so much time in Brussels, and see all they could from the train.

At Oberwinter, where there is the finest view down the Rhine, all the party looked back to see it.

Coblence was the next large town, and the situation is beautiful, as it is at the confluence of the Rhine and the Moselle, with the strong fortifications opposite, the Castle of Ehrenbreitstein, often called the Gibraltar of the Rhine.

Just after leaving Coblence they saw two castles, one the royal castle of Stolzenfels on its "proud rock," more than four hundred feet above the river. It was destroyed by the French in the seventeenth century, but is now completely restored.

The other castle is directly opposite, above the mouth of the Lahn river, is called the Castle of Lahneck, and has been lately restored. Alice knew the legend of this castle, and told it to the rest of the party.

"It was here, in the beginning of the fourteenth century, that the order of Knights Templars, which had been founded for religious purposes chiefly, was severely persecuted by Philippe le Beau of France and Pope Clement V.

"After many vicissitudes there was a long and

LAHNECK CASTLE. — *Page 54.*

desperate siege, in which all the knights fell except one man. He held the commander at bay, who was so overpowered by the knight's bravery he offered him life and liberty if he would stop fighting and beg for mercy.

"The templar's only answer was to throw his spear among the soldiers, and then was killed by throwing himself on their lances."

Boppart was the next town of any interest, it being a walled town of Roman origin.

The wall had crumbled away in many places, and houses had been built on the ruins.

On the opposite side of the river was Bornhoffen, with its twin castles of Sternberg and Liebenstein, or "The Brothers."

Mr. Winter told this legend, which runs that once a rich knight, with his two sons and one daughter, lived there, and were very rich in gold and lands, which the old knight had gained through wrong and robbery. All his neighbors felt sure that such ill-gotten wealth would bring him anything but blessings.

The brothers inherited the avarice of the father: but the sister was lovely and gentle, like her mother. When the father died the brothers gave

their sister much less than a third of the property.
She gave hers to the cause of religion and went
into a convent.

The brothers, disappointed, disputed over their
share, and at last fell in love with the same
maiden, who did not hesitate to flirt with both
and increase their jealousy. They finally fought and
killed each other.

Just as Mr. Winter finished his story, the guard
of the train put his head into the car window, to
say that the Lorely rock was nearly in sight.

CHAPTER VIII.

THE LEGEND OF THE LORELY.

BOTH girls jumped to their feet, for of course they were interested to see that famous rock where the water-nymph Lore was said to have lived. She would appear on the top of the rock, clothed in wonderful garments, and a veil of the color of the sea-green water reaching to her feet, to lure wicked people to destruction by her singing.

The people who came to the foot of the rock were swallowed in the waves. while those who tried to climb to the top were either thrown back into the water or led through the dense woods. only to be days finding their way out of them.

Lore was very kind to good people. having the fairy power of distinguishing good from evil.

At last a young count, much to his father's un-happiness. saw and fell in love with her. He constantly went to gaze upon her, for she was very beautiful.

He used to carry his zither and play and sing to her, until she finally caused the waves to rise so high that his boat was upset and broken. The count sank into the waves, and his attendants returned home to tell the father the sad news.

The old count swore revenge, and was going to seize Lore and have her burnt. The next night he took some friends and surrounded the rock.

When Lore appeared the old count said, " Where is my son ? "

Lore pointed to the waves, at the same time continuing to sing very sweetly.

As soon as Lore had finished her song, she threw a stone into the river, which caused a wave to rise. She mounted it and sank from view with it, never to be seen again, though her singing was often heard by men passing by.

The rock was formerly called Lorely, but is now Lurlei, and has a lovely echo said to be the gift of Lore.

The girls were disappointed to see the water around the rock so very quiet — no whirlpool at all.

When they saw that a cut had been made through the rock for railroad trains, all the romance was gone for them.

Alice said. "O papa, how could anybody spoil that pretty story by running trains through the rock? If that is the way my romances are going to end I will not read any more."

However, she soon saw a house built in the river, and wanted to know what it was and why it was there.

"I know," said Nellie. "I was reading about it the other day."

It is called the Pfalz, and was built by Louis of Bavaria in the thirteenth century, in order to exact tribute from passing vessels.

Opposite is the town of Bacharach, the Ara Bacchi of the Romans, and has long been famous for its wines. In Longfellow's "Golden Legend" is the old rhyme, —

> "At Bacharach on the Rhine,
> At Hochheim on the Main,
> And at Würzburg on the Stein,
> Grow the three best kinds of wine."

The Bacchus-Altar is to be found in this lovely country. It stands just below the town, but the water has to be very low to read the inscription (which is nearly illegible), as it is situated between the bank of the river and an islet.

The Altar is supposed to have been erected by the Romans to their god of wine.

Many other castles, some restored, but the most of them in ruins, were passed, before Assmanshausen, famous for its red wines, was reached.

Mr. Winter said, "Now this ends what is called 'the great gorge of the Rhine,' and the river will broaden, and the open country, not very interesting, is before you."

Just before reaching Bingen they saw the ruins of Ehrenfels, and in the middle of the river the Mausthurm, or "Mouse Tower."

"O papa, I know the story of that tower," said Alice. "Can I tell it?"

"We are only too glad to hear it," said her mamma.

"Hatto was Bishop of Fulda, and wishing to be

MOUSE TOWER. — *Page* 61.

made Archbishop of Mayence, used every means in his power to accomplish his purpose. He succeeded, and became very ambitious, proud, and cruel. He taxed the poor to build for himself fine dwellings.

"At last he built the tower in the river where it was very narrow, to compel all ships to pay him toll.

"A famine set in, and he, having plenty of money, bought up everything and filled his granaries. He sold his stores at such high prices that only the rich could buy.

"He paid no heed to the supplications of the famishing people, as he intended building a superb palace with his money.

"One day when Hatto was entertaining friends at dinner, the starving people forced their way into the dining-hall and begged for food. He told them to go to a large barn where corn should be given them. When they were all inside, Hatto ordered the doors to be closed and fastened on the outside and the barn to be set on fire.

"When their shrieks reached the dining-hall, Hatto turned to his guests and said, 'Hear how the corn-mice squeal: I do the same to rebels as I do to them.'

"The wrath of Heaven was turned against him, for out of the ashes at the barn thousands of mice took their way to the palace, filling the rooms and attacking Hatto. Thousands were killed, but they steadily increased. and he was finally obliged to flee in terror of his life to a boat. still pursued by legions.

"Hatto was ferried over the Rhine to the tower, but the mice perforated the walls. and fell on him by the thousands. and ate him up. They then disappeared, and the tower has been called the 'Mouse Tower' ever since.

"It has never been used in any way, but stands as a warning to despotic people."

Mr. Winter said, "Alice. you told that very well; but he was not such a very wicked man as the legend makes him. He was imperious and caused his people much suffering. but was the Emperor's confidant and was called the 'Heart of the King.'"

Bingen is not a very interesting town, but has many walks and drives that are full of interest in every way.

Directly opposite, on the heights of Niederwald, is the beautiful monument built to commemorate the restitution of the German Empire in 1870–1871.

Alice and Nellie did wish they could stop long enough to go up and see it. it looked so grand and

mighty outlined against the sky. Mr. Winter said,
"No, we must get to Mayence to-night."

There was not much of interest after leaving
Bingen, as the train left the river and the Rhine was
not seen again until just before entering Mayence,
where the Main flows most peacefully into it, making
a very beautiful picture.

CHAPTER IX.

MR. WINTER as usual had telegraphed to Mayence for rooms, and found very comfortable,
large rooms ready for them in a new, pleasant hotel
near the station.

After resting a little while Mr. Winter said, "Who
wants to go with me and take a drive around the
city ?"

The entire party, even Mrs. Winter. who had
thought she was too tired to go out again, said they
would like to go.

What a delightful drive they had. at the close of
a warm. lovely day. around that interesting old city.
with its wonderful fortifications! The view of the
rivers at the base of the hill they thought as pretty
as any they had seen all day.

Mr. Winter told them what a very old city it was,

MAYENCE.—GENERAL VIEW.—*Page 65.*

a Roman camp having been laid there thirty-eight years before Christ.

The foundations may be said to date from fourteen years B.C., when Drusus built his extensive fortifications. There is a Roman monument forty-five feet high erected in honor of Drusus. There are also remains of a Roman aqueduct to be found outside the city.

The cathedral was founded in 798. It has been burnt and restored six times, and is one of the grandest in Germany.

Just outside the cathedral they saw a fine statue of Gutenberg, who is regarded by the Germans as the inventor of movable types for printing.

Our party drove back to the hotel, had a nice supper, which was waiting for them, and went to bed feeling they had enjoyed that day more than any since leaving home.

The next morning all were rested and eager to get to Nuremberg, the end of the trip. Mr. Winter, by some mistake, did not get the fast train, and as the one they took stopped very often, and the scenery was not very interesting, our party arrived in Nuremberg so tired they ate their supper and went directly to bed.

CHAPTER X.

NUREMBERG.

IN the morning Mr. Winter said, "I will give one day to you for sight-seeing, and then I must attend to business. You will have to spend the rest of your time going around with a guide or by yourselves."

Alice was delighted with the old moat which was opposite her window, and wanted to look in it at once.

Nellie felt the castle was of more importance, and could hardly wait to get there. The moat surrounds the old city, and now is rented to gardeners, who live in the old towers and cultivate the land in the moat.

Our party started out to walk until they were tired, and kept on the sidewalk side of the moat, and thought it did look so pretty with everything

NUREMBERG WALLS.

so fresh and green. The cherry-trees were all white with their lovely blossoms, which grew even with the sidewalk.

Finally they went through an old gateway. which was said to be the one where a rope was kept in the olden time. to use on the bakers. If they did

not give full weight, the bakers were tied to the
end of a pole and dipped into the water several
times. If poison was found in the bread, they were
immediately drowned.

As the ladies were getting tired, Mr. Winter called
a carriage to drive them to the castle. As he
could speak German, the driver told him many interesting things, and pointed out various objects of
interest. He showed them one house that had been
occupied by the same family for four hundred and
fifty years.

The churches of St. Sebald and St. Lawrence they
admired very much on the outside, leaving the
beauties of the interiors for another day. They
passed one fountain called the Goose Man, and
another, the Beautiful Fountain, built in 1385. Also,
a fine statue of Hans Sachs, erected in 1874, who
was known through Germany as the cobbler-poet.
It was from his life Wagner wrote the opera of the
" Meistersinger."

Soon the driver drew up his horses at a corner
where a small house stood under a hill, called the

ALBRECHT DÜRER'S HOUSE. — *Page* 74.

Sausage Shop, for its wonderfully cooked sausages. It has been made famous by such men as Albert Dürer, the great artist, Hans Sachs, and the old bergomasters meeting there for their nightly mugs of beer and a sausage.

The statue of Albert Dürer, erected in 1840, is between the Sausage Shop and his old home. All the houses, with their deep, slanting roofs, were objects of interest, but most of all was that of Albert Dürer, which is the only house in Nuremberg that has not undergone some alteration.

The house is now filled with many curiosities, some of them having belonged to Albert Dürer, and is open every day to visitors. The girls wanted to stop and go in at once, but Mr. Winter said, " No, we cannot stop now; we must get to the castle, and leave the house until we have more time."

The castle stands very high, and they were obliged to drive up through very narrow and steep streets; but the horses were used to it, and Mrs. Winter finally overcame her nervousness.

When the top of the hill was reached, there was

a plateau where a beautiful view of the city was to be seen. They left the carriage here, and after

NUREMBERG CASTLE.

looking at the scenery they walked on up to the castle.

On the way they saw a small shed, and, on looking in, found it held the famous well. A young girl was there, who, in a parrot sort of way, told them that the well was built in the eleventh century. under Conrad II.. by convicts, and that it took thirty years to finish it. She told Mrs. Winter to hold a mirror in her hand while she lowered a candle, to show by the reflection in the mirror the depth of the well. It took just six seconds for water which she poured out of a glass to reach the water in the well. She told them it was four hundred and fifty feet deep. and they all believed her.

In the courtyard of the castle they saw an old linden tree growing, which is said ʼto have been planted by Empress Runigunde eight hundred years ago.

The castle they found quite interesting without being very elegant. A lady in charge of it told them many things of interest about the castle and the city.

She told them that the first records of Nuremberg date from 1050. In 1105 the town was besieged. conquered, and destroyed by Henry V., again besieged in 1127 by Emperor Lothar, from which time imperial officials appeared who took the title of Burggrafer.

Frederick I. (Barbarossa), under whom the burg was enlarged, frequently lived here from 1156 to 1188. Rudolph von Hapsburg held his first diet here in 1274, and often visited the town.

Under Emperor Karl IV. the first stone bridge was built. and the streets were paved.

The first fundamental law of the empire was formed by him. and is known as the "Golden Bull." It was framed in Nuremberg in 1356, and is still kept in Frankfort.

According to this law, every German emperor was obliged to spend his first day of government in Nuremberg.

His government was very favorable to Nuremberg in every way.

The four large towers were built 1555 to 1568, after a plan designed by Albert Dürer. The town reached its highest artistic development in the fifteenth and sixteenth centuries. under such men as Albert Dürer, A. Krafft, Herman Fischer. and many others.

Goblets and many such objects of art were made here at that time. In 1649 Nuremberg displayed its last splendor. Commerce had been ruined by different wars. In 1806 it was made a matter of rejoicing when it came under the crown of Bavaria. King Ludwig first revived art, and trade made a start.

In 1835 the first railroad was opened to Firth. In 1855 King Max II. with his family lived here, and the Imperial Burg was offered to him as a present by the town.

The lady also told them that the five-cornered tower, which is the oldest building in Nuremberg and connected with the castle, contained a collection of instruments of torture. Among them is the iron virgin, a figure of a woman. which opens and is full of spikes. The poor victim would be shut up in its clutches.

None of our party felt like visiting that horrible place, so they thanked the woman, and took some last looks at the beautiful views to be seen from the windows. To their surprise they found it was

noon-time, and as everything in Nuremberg is closed
for an hour and a half at mid-day, they were
driven back to the Wurtemberger Hof, their comfortable hotel, where everything possible was done
for their pleasure.

After a good dinner and a rest, Mr. Winter said
he thought, as his time was so limited, he would
like to visit the Town Hall and St. John's Cemetery. A guide was found, and they started out with
more enthusiasm than ever.

The guide told them that the Town Hall was
built in the years from 1616 to 1619, in Italian
style. He pointed out to them a fine picture by
Paul Ritter, painted in 1882, to represent the act
of the arrival of the German Emperor's Insignia in
Nuremberg. The guide also showed them several
pictures of Dürer's representing the triumphal pro-
cession of Emperor Maximilian. His pictures are,
many of them, very indistinct.

They were taken into a room where the wedding
couples go to sign their marriage contracts.

Mr. Winter was more interested than the girls,

and Mrs. Winter was so tired they were glad
enough to get in the carriage and be driven to the
famous old cemetery.

For some blocks before reaching the entrance are
paintings of Christ, representing the last days of his
life.

At the gateway are the three statues of Christ
and the two thieves nailed to the cross.

The guide showed them the graves of Dürer and
Sachs, and one of a man who had been killed,
while asleep, by his wife hammering a nail in his
head. There was a bronze skull, with the nail in
it just where she killed him.

Another interesting bronze was the figure of a
woman with a lizard on a perch, which, when
touched, turns towards the woman's figure and shows
where she was bitten in the neck by the lizard
that killed her.

The girls thought that very quaint and more
interesting than any they saw, though there were
many very beautifully carved, and, being of bronze,
were of great value.

While our party was wandering through the cemetery a funeral was taking place, and as the entire service was intoned, it was very impressive.

Mr. Winter said as they entered the carriage, "You have had enough sight-seeing for to-day, and we will drive home and talk over all the wonderful and interesting things we have seen and heard to-day."

NUREMBERG.

CHAPTER XI.

NUREMBERG. — *Continued.*

THE following morning Mr. Winter left the ladies, who walked aimlessly. not caring much where they went. it was all so full of interest to them.

Accidentally they visited quite an interesting place called the Preller House. It was built three hundred years ago by a Venetian nobleman, and is now used as a furniture warehouse. There is a chapel in it, and some of the old furniture still remains.

The ceilings are very fine, and in two of the rooms were only discovered when the present occupants were having gas-pipes put in the house.

Mr. Winter did not come home to dinner, and in the afternoon Mrs. Winter and the girls went to the Museum, where they found more to interest them than anywhere they had been. It had a very large and interesting collection of paintings and antiquities, but the girls enjoyed seeing the old cloister — the first they had ever seen.

That evening when Mr. Winter came home, he told his wife that he should only be obliged to remain one more day, and they must entertain themselves again without him.

The next morning Mrs. Winter took a guide with them, as she wished to visit some of the shops where they could collect some curiosities.

They also went to the Market square, where the poor people can buy everything they need at very reasonable prices.

Mrs. Winter then said, "Now, girls, we will visit those churches of which we have only seen the outside."

The guide took them first to St. Lawrence's Church.

This church, he told them, was mentioned as early as 1006, and had the handsomest artistic decoration of any of the celebrated churches throughout Germany. The finest portion is the choir, with a vaulted roof supported by slender pillars from which the arches are formed like palm branches.

The guide wished them particularly to look at the Gothic bronze chandelier, which weighs four hundred and eighty-two pounds, and was cast by Peter Vischer in 1489.

The girls were charmed by the seven windows of the choir, which are considered the best examples of Nuremberg glass-painting from 1450 to 1490. The last window, called the Emperor's, was presented by the citizens of Nuremberg in memory of the restitution of the German Empire. It was put in the 22d of March, 1881. Mrs. Winter was much interested in some beautiful tapestries representing the lives of St. Lawrence and St. Catharine, and are over four hundred years old.

There were many more paintings of much interest, some of them Albert Dürer's. As they were leaving, the girls saw some richly carved chairs by the doors, and asked the guide why they were there.

He told them that they formerly belonged to the guilds, and the masters sat in them, in turn, to receive alms.

From this church our party was driven to St. Sebaldus's, which was finished in the tenth century. One of the most interesting things they saw was the font, which was remarkable not only as the first product of Nuremberg's foundries, but as having been used to christen King Wenceslas of Bohemia, in 1361.

There were more paintings of Dürer's to be seen here, but the finest work was the sepulchre of St. Sebaldus in the centre of the choir. It is the most extensive work German art has ever produced, and was cast by Peter Vischer and his five sons.

"It was commenced in 1508 and completed in 1519. It rests on twelve snails, having four dolphins at its corners. the whole forming a pagan temple adorned with the Twelve Apostles. It is surmounted by twelve smaller figures, and finally by an infant Christ holding a globus in his hand, the latter being a key of the whole monument, when it is to be rent asunder. There is also a fine portrait of Peter Vischer in this church."

Of course there were many more objects of interest to be seen, but Mrs. Winter thought they had seen enough; so they were driven home to dinner.

In the afternoon they took a drive out of the city to a beer-garden situated at the side of a pretty lake. They had some tea, and walked on the borders of the lake quite a distance. Mrs. Winter said, "I wish we had such a quiet, pretty place near home where we could spend an afternoon as delightfully as we have here."

That evening Nellie said, "Dear Mrs. Winter, how can I ever thank you and your husband for this trip? Mamma could not have come, and never shall I forget what I have enjoyed through your kindness."

Mrs. Winter told her that the pleasure she had given them was more than hers, as it had added so much to Alice's happiness.

Alice said, "Now, mamma, will you not add to our pleasures by repeating Longfellow's beautiful poem on Nuremberg before we go to bed?"

"Dear Mrs. Winter, please do," said Nellie. "I have never heard of it, but I know it must be very lovely."

"Very well," said Mrs. Winter. "I certainly never knew a more appropriate time to recite it than now."

The girls gathered around her in the twilight as she sweetly commenced:—

In the valley of the Pegnitz, where
    across broad meadow-lands
Rise the blue Franconian mountains,
    Nuremberg, the ancient, stands.

Quaint old town of toil and traffic,
    quaint old town of art and song,
Memories haunt thy pointed gables,
    like the rooks that round them
    throng:

Memories of the Middle Ages,
    when the emperors, rough and
    bold,
Had their dwelling in the castle, time
    defying, centuries old;

And thy brave and thrifty burghers
    boasted, in their uncouth rhyme,
That their great imperial city stretched
    its hand through every clime.

In the courtyard of the castle, bound
  with many an iron band,
Stands the mighty linden planted by
  Queen Cunigunde's hand;

On the square the oriel window,
  where in old heroic days
Sat the poet Melchior singing Kaiser
  Maximilian's praise.

Everywhere I see around me rise
  the wondrous world of Art —
Fountains wrought with richest sculpture standing in the common
  mart:

And above cathedral doorways saints
  and bishops carved in stone,
By a former age commissioned as
  apostles to our own.

In the church of sainted Sebald sleeps
  enshrined his holy dust,
And in bronze the Twelve Apostles
  guard from age to age their
  trust;

In the church of sainted Lawrence
  stands a pix of sculpture rare,

Like the foamy sheaf of fountains,
  rising through the painted air.

Here, when Art was still religion,
  with a simple, reverent heart,
Lived and labored Albrecht Dürer,
  the Evangelist of Art:

Hence in silence and in sorrow, toil-
  ing still with busy hand,
Like an emigrant he wandered, seek-
  ing for the Better Land;

Emigravit is the inscription on the
  tombstone where he lies;
Dead he is not, but departed, — for
  the artist never dies.

Fairer seems the ancient city, and the
  sunshine seems more fair,
That he once has trod its pavement,
  that he once has breathed its air.

Through these streets, so broad and
  stately, these obscure and dis-
  mal lanes,
Walked of yore the Mastersingers,
  chanting rude poetic strains.

From remote and sunless suburbs came
　they to the friendly guild,
Building nests in Fame's great temple,
　as in spouts the swallows build.

As the weaver plied the shuttle, wove
　he too the mystic rhyme,
And the smith his iron measures ham-
　mered to the anvil's chime;

Thanking God, whose boundless wis-
　dom makes the flowers of
　poesy bloom
In the forge's dust and cinders, in
　the tissues of the loom.

Here Hans Sachs, the cobbler-poet,
　laureate of the gentle craft,
Wisest of the Twelve Wise Mas-
　ters, in huge folios sang and
　laughed;

But his house is now an ale-house,
　with a nicely sanded floor,
And a garland in the window, and
　his face above the door;

Painted by some humble artist, as in
　Adam Puschman's song,

As the old man, gray and dove-like,
　with his great beard white and
　long,
And at night the swart mechanic comes
　to drown his cash and care,
Quaffing ale from pewter tankards,
　in the master's antique chair.

Vanished is the ancient splendor, and
　before my dreamy eye
Wave these mingling shapes and fig-
　ures, like a faded tapestry.

Not thy councils, not thy Kaisers, win
　for thee the world's regard;
But thy painter, Albrecht Dürer, and
　Hans Sachs thy cobbler-bard.

Thus, O Nuremberg, a wanderer
　from a region far away,
As he paced thy streets and court-
　yards, sang in thought his
　careless lay;

Gathering from the pavement's crev-
　ice, as a floweret of the soil,
The nobility of labor — the long
　pedigree of toil.

"How very beautiful!" said Nellie. "Thank you so much, Mrs. Winter, for reciting it to us. I shall learn it myself when I get home, trusting I may sometime give as much pleasure to another as you have given me."

Mr. Winter said, "Why. Agnes, I never heard you recite that poem so well."

"I never did," said his wife; "for I never truly felt it before."

"Thank you, mamma dear." said Alice. "Now we will go to bed. feeling all the happier for the lovely poem which has put our best thoughts into words."

STRASBOURG CATHEDRAL—SIDE VIEW.

CHAPTER XII.

STRASBOURG.

MRS. WINTER was very anxious to travel to Paris by the way of Strasbourg, as she had always wished to see the cathedral with its wonderful clock.

Mr. Winter made inquiries and found that was decidedly the best way to go, which was a great delight to them all.

Our party left Nuremberg early in the morning, sorry to see the last of the most interesting city they had seen thus far on their trip. Nellie, who was looking forward to meeting her father and mother in Paris, was quite happy to make a move in that direction.

The first part of the trip was not very interesting, but the latter was delightful, and as they had a compartment to themselves the girls could enjoy the view from both sides of the train. A change of cars was made at a place where there was hardly anything but the station and the railroad interests. Here they ate a cold lunch from the counter, though there were some hot dishes on a table; but they did not look very tempting.

The spire of the Strasbourg Cathedral could be seen some time before reaching the station, and well it might, being four hundred and sixty-six feet high, and by some authorities said to be the highest in the world.

The fortifications had been so fine at Mayence our party was surprised to find others much finer

here, many of them being new, having been built
at the time of the French and German war in
1870.

The engineering of some of them is particularly
fine, as they are made to be opened, so that all the
surrounding country can be flooded if necessary.

The train wound round the city, giving them a
fine view of the fortifications and the soldiers being
drilled in many of the enclosures.

Strasbourg was one of the most important cities
during the last war, and a great portion of it was
destroyed. One side of the cathedral was badly
damaged, but is now thoroughly restored.

Mr. Winter took his family to a small hotel on
the square near the station, having been recommended there by the manager of the hotel at Nuremberg. He found it very comfortable, and every
possible attention was shown them.

Arriving about five o'clock, there was plenty of
time to be driven around the city. Of course they
started for the cathedral, but on the way the driver
stopped the carriage to point out one of the highest

chimneys on one of the tallest houses, where the storks had built a nest.

He also told them how the storks arrive every spring and build their nests, and then leave in the fall with their young, to return the next spring with their families no larger nor smaller than when they go away. What becomes of the surplus is a great question—whether they only increase sufficiently to fill the vacancies caused by death or old age, or that the young ones found colonies in other countries.

The storks are held in great reverence by mankind, and are never harmed. Indeed, it is considered good fortune to the inmates of a house when a nest is built on one of its chimneys.

The driver told a story of one man who gave up the use of his room an entire winter, rather than destroy a nest which two storks had built over the top of his chimney, and thus prevented his building a fire.

As they approached the cathedral Alice said, "Why, papa, where is the clock? I cannot see it at all."

STRASBOURG STORKS. — *Page* 94.

"I do not know," said Mr. Winter; "but it certainly is there somewhere."

The driver took them to the front of the building, where they were met by a guide, who showed them the beauties of the outside architecture and the many statues of the apostles and saints. He told them that the cathedral was commenced in 1015 and finished in 1601.

The guide showed them the plateau half-way up the height of the steeple, and told them that it is used by men who watch for fires all the time. The citizens are so proud of the cathedral that they have it dusted and washed inside very frequently.

"Where is the clock?" said Mrs. Winter, as soon as the guide stopped talking long enough for her to speak a word.

The man did not answer, but took them around to a side door, where, after receiving his tip, he left them and walked away.

At first they did not know what to do, but Mrs. Winter said, "I think we had better go inside if we can."

In they went, and right by the door was the clock. A fine-looking man dressed elegantly met

STRASBOURG—CATHEDRAL CLOCK. — *Page 96.*

them. He proved to be a finely educated Swiss, and he explained the various wonders of the clock.

He told them that the clock was built three hundred years ago, and was to run a certain number of years. It shows all fête days for all those years. tells the changes of the moon, eclipses — in fact. everything that one could imagine.

The apostles do not all come out and walk around except at noon, but as it was quarter before six our party saw three men move.

The clock stops at six at night and then commences again at six in the morning.

Mrs. Winter said the longer she looked at it, the more wonderful it seemed to her that any man could think of so many things.

The guide also told them that the man who first conceived the idea of the clock became totally blind when it was nearly completed. Of course he could work no more, and it was never thought the clock would be finished.

He lived thirty years. and after his death another man was found who thought he could complete it.

He succeeded, and was paid by the government for his time and work.

Mrs. Winter said, "I think it is the most wonderful thing I ever saw, and I do not know which man I admire the most — the one who conceived such a work, or the man who could carry out such marvellous thoughts of a man whom he had never met."

After leaving the cathedral our party was driven around the city. The old part they found very quaint and picturesque, with its high and sloping roofs. The new part, built by the Germans, was very handsome, some of the buildings, like the palace, conservatory of music, and the post-office, being particularly fine.

The driver told them that one of the great interests there was the making of *pâté de foie gras*. It is made from the livers of geese which are fed in such a way that the liver grows abnormally large, often weighing three pounds.

He also told them that many of the French people are still very bitter against the Germans, even pulling down their shades to the windows if a regiment should march by the house.

On their return to the hotel, the manager told Mr. Winter he would have a very quick and comfortable journey to Paris if he took the Orient express which runs between Constantinople and Paris. It would leave Strasbourg three hours later than the ordinary train, and would arrive in Paris some hours before it.

Mr. Winter engaged a compartment at once, and the next day had a very enjoyable trip, though it was a very long one. The first part of the route, over mountains and through ravines, was very delightful; but after getting into France it was flat and uninteresting.

They passed through Epérgny, which was interesting for its vines, which covered the fields for many miles. From these grapes champagne is made.

Paris was reached at six o'clock, and their hotel, which had been recommended by friends, was found to be very homelike.

The Fords were there waiting for them, and were as glad to see Nellie as she was glad to be with them again.

CHAPTER XIII.

HOMEWARD BOUND.

THAT evening after Nellie had told her mamma some of her pleasant experiences. Mr. Winter said, " Now we have just five days to spend in Paris, and you must decide what you would most like to do. Mr. Ford and I are entirely at your disposal."

Guidebooks were brought out and studied, and after many discussions their plans were settled for each day.

On Thursday morning they went to the Louvre, feeling there would be so many pictures to see they had better visit it first.

How tired they did get sliding around on those slippery floors, trying to see the nine miles of pictures, many of which were quite uninteresting to them all.

In the afternoon Mr. Winter took his wife and

the girls in a carriage, and started for the Bois de
Boulogne. When the Place de la Concorde was
reached, with its monolithic obelisk of Luxor, and

PLACE DE LA CONCORDE.

fountains and statues, with the gardens of the
Tuileries one side, and the Champs Élysées on the
other, the girls both exclaimed, " How beautiful! "
but Nellie added, " When I think of all the horrors
that have taken place here it loses some of its love-
liness to me."

The drive through the Champs Élysées they thought very beautiful, and when they reached the Arc de Triomphe de l'Étoile, the most beautiful in the world, their admiration knew no bounds.

Mr. Winter said, "Alice, what do you know about this?"

Alice answered that "It was commenced by Napoleon I. in 1806 and finished by Louis Philippe, and cost over two millions of dollars. It is about one hundred and fifty feet high, and the same in breadth, and the central arch is ninety feet high."

"Very good, my dear; you know that lesson very well," said her papa.

From there to the Bois everything was full of interest to them, and the drive around the Cascade Alice thought particularly lovely.

Nellie said, "It is not kept up as nicely as I like to see a park. They had better make Central Park a visit, and see its nicely cut lawns and trimmed bushes."

On their way home they were driven through the Place Vendôme, with its magnificent column in the centre.

Nellie said, "I can tell you a little about that, Mr. Winter, if you would like me to."

"Of course I should," said Mr. Winter.

"It is one hundred and forty feet high, and was also built by Napoleon I. It was pulled down by the Communists in 1871, but has since been restored."

The girls felt quite at home historically in Paris, as all these interesting things were very fresh in their minds.

In the evening, being very near the Palais Royale, which was built for Cardinal Richelieu, they thought it would be a pleasant way to pass their evening to go and walk around and gaze into the shop windows. The ladies were too tired, so the gentlemen took the girls, and they had a delightful time. Alice told her mamma on her return that she enjoyed it, but did not care to go again; she had seen so much jewelry, all alike, that it was actually tiresome.

Friday morning they drove to the Palais du Luxembourg, which has been prison, palace, senate-house, and is now noted for its sculptures and paintings.

Our party enjoyed it much more than the Louvre, as the paintings were so many of them modern and very familiar to them.

At the back of the garden they saw the statue of Marshal Ney. on the very spot where he was shot.

Being on that side of the river. they visited the Church of the Hôtel des Invalides to see the tomb of Napoleon I. It was directly under the dome, and the softened lights all around made it very beautiful.

After being driven home and having lunch, they walked to the Madeleine. the most magnificent of modern churches.

Mrs. Winter said. " This is very beautiful, but I do like the solemnity of some of the older churches I have seen very much better."

Leaving there, they walked through some of those wide and interesting boulevards, watching the people and carriages and gazing into the fascinating shop-windows.

Mr. Ford said. "I thought I had seen in New

York some florists' windows that could not be improved, but I find I was mistaken. Never have I seen such windows as these."

When too tired to walk any farther, carriages were called, and they were driven to the Cathedral of Notre Dame, built on an island in the Seine; from there to the Panthéon, which Alice said "looked like a barn, and was cold and inhospitable."

The most interesting thing about it was, that such celebrated men as Victor Hugo, Marat, Voltaire, Mirabeau, and Rousseau had been buried there. The Hôtel de Ville, recently restored, they passed on their way home.

The evening was given to the Hippodrome, which is quite the thing to do in Paris, and is wonderfully fine.

The drive there was like a picture of fairyland, with the bright lights and trees and glimpses of the river.

Saturday was devoted to shopping, a great deal of it being done at the Magasin de Louvre and the Bon Marché. The buildings are immense, and there is everything to be found in them that one could possibly desire.

That evening it was decided to go to the opera at the Grand Opera House, the most beautiful one in the world. The girls were so excited they could not eat any dinner, for it was their first appearance.

Faust was the opera given, and a wonderful ballet followed it. Between the opera and ballet they all went outside and looked down at the men on horseback, stationed like sentinels outside the building.

Before them was the whole length of the Rue de l'Opera a blaze of light. Alice said, "Nothing yet has been as delightful as this evening."

Sunday was bright and clear, much to the delight of our sight-seers, as they were going to Versailles. They decided on Sunday, as the fountains were advertised to play, and all were very anxious to see them.

They drove there and enjoyed every moment, especially when passing St. Cloud. They saw all it was possible to see in one day, but felt as if it was very little, after all.

They went through the palace as fast as they could, but any one knows who has been there that with those glossy floors it took time.

The room devoted to war pictures they did not care for, but were much interested in Marie Antoinette's private rooms, which were so very small, and also in the place where the Swiss Guards were killed in defending her.

The state apartments were very elegant, especially the Galerie de Glace, where the German emperor was proclaimed emperor in the late war.

Of course the girls were eager to get to the Great and Little Trianon. They were disappointed in the size and simplicity of their furnishings. The rooms, however, were so full of historical interest that their disappointment was forgotten, and they thought they could have spent all their time in the two houses.

In the coach-house were seen some very curious old state coaches used by Charles X. and Napoleon I. and many other sovereigns.

The man in charge was almost as much of a

PETIT TRIANON. - *Page* 108.

curiosity as the coaches. he told his stories in such
an interesting manner. laughing heartily at his own
jokes.

The drive home was delightful. but they were all
too tired to say very much. After a good dinner,
the two girls talked as fast as magpies over the
delights of the day. Being like most girls. Marie

Antoinette was one of the most interesting characters in French history, and they talked of her and her sad life, feeling almost as if they had lived a portion of it with her, in the quiet retreat and lovely gardens of Versailles.

Mr. Winter said to his wife, "I have really finished my business this side of the water, and unless you would like to remain in London three or four more days for the 'Etruria,' we can catch the 'Teutonic' next Wednesday."

Mrs. Winter said she would like to go home on the "Teutonic" very much, but did not like to leave Mr. and Mrs. Ford, as they had made all their arrangements to go home together.

Mr. Ford said, " We are delighted to shorten the trip, as I ought to be at home now; but we did not like to break up the party."

" Very well," said Mr. Winter. " We will go out and telegraph to Liverpool for state-rooms."

Alice said to her mamma, " I wonder if we can like the 'Teutonic' as well as we did the 'Etruria' that brought us over the seas so safely."

Monday was devoted to visiting the Salon, where they saw so many pictures that they came away with a very vague idea of what they had seen, but all agreed they preferred the English pictures of the present day to those of the French.

Tuesday night saw our party again in London, but at the Savoy Hotel. where they had delightful rooms overlooking the river.

Wednesday at eleven o'clock our happy party took the special train which connects with the fast steamers, and at four o'clock were on the " Teutonic " and starting for home.

A lovely night down to Queenstown. where the steamer stops for the mails. While waiting the next morning, Mr. Winter and Mr. Ford took Alice and Nellie on shore in the tug. and gave them a nice drive in a jaunting car.

The girls did not enjoy the drive very much, but were glad of the experience.

The ladies were very much interested in the boats which came out to the " Teutonic " with women who had laces and small articles to sell. The things

were sent up to the deck in baskets, on ropes,
which were tossed up for the passengers to catch.

THAMES EMBANKMENT. — *Page* 111.

Some of the Irish girls were very bright, and made
very good sales.

At last the tug with the mails arrived, and was

attached to the steamer at once. Both went down the harbor until the passengers, among them our party, and the mails had been transferred. The girls were uneasy until they were with their mothers.

At two o'clock the tug left them, and then, indeed, it seemed as if they had started for home.

One bad stormy day, some foggy and some delightful ones, fell to their share. No one of their party was sick, and they thought the steamer delightful. Much as they had liked the " Etruria," it was decided by all that the " Teutonic" would be their steamer in the future.

New York was reached on Wednesday afternoon, and at night the entire party was at the Fifth Avenue Hotel, feeling very glad to get safely across the ocean again. They had become such good friends it was very hard to separate.

However, a promise was made by the Fords to visit Mr. and Mr. Winter before the summer was over.

Thursday night the Winters could have been found in their own home, all very happy, and feeling that

the following years would be fuller of interest in
every way for the experiences, most of them pleasant, of their charming trip to Nuremberg and
back.